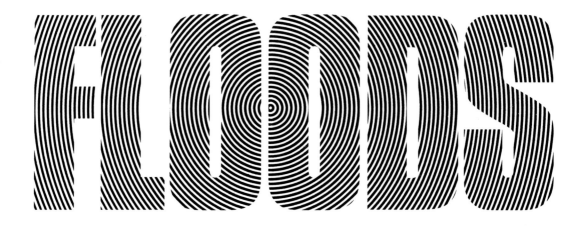

FLOODS

Aleksandrs Rozens

TWENTY-FIRST CENTURY BOOKS

A Division of Henry Holt and Company
New York

Twenty-First Century Books
A division of Henry Holt and Company, Inc.
115 West 18th Street
New York, New York 10011

Henry Holt® and colophon are trademarks of Henry Holt and
Company, Inc.
Publishers since 1866

Published in Canada by Fitzhenry & Whiteside Ltd.
195 Allstate Parkway, Markham, Ontario L3R 4T8

Printed in the United States of America

All first editions are printed on acid-free paper ∞.

Created and produced in association with Blackbirch Graphics, Inc.

This one is for Frank Coffey

Acknowledgments
The author would like to thank Rocky Lopes of the American Red Cross,
William Kovari, Jr., of the Goodard Institute of Space Studies, Bruce
Levy who assisted with research, and Frank Coffey for his editorial
advice.

Library of Congress Cataloging-in-Publication Data

Rozens, Aleksandrs, 1967–
    Floods / Aleksandrs Rozens. — 1st ed.
        p.   cm. — (When disaster strikes)
    Includes index.
    ISBN 0-8050-3097-2 (acid-free)
    1. Floods—Juvenile literature. [1. Floods.] I. Title. II. Series.
GB 1399.R69   1994
363.3'493—dc20
                                                                93-39832
                                                                    CIP
                                                                     AC

Contents

Tragedy Near St. Louis

During the summer of 1993, record rainfall soaked many parts of the midwestern United States. Seven weeks of nearly solid rain bloated the Mississippi River and its major tributaries, or branches, to record levels. Farm fields in the region looked like lakes, and soybean and corn crops had to be left unplanted. Farm equipment was buried in mud. Towns and cities nestled along the Mississippi River were ravaged by its powerful waters. In downtown areas of St. Louis, Missouri; Memphis, Tennessee; and Helena, Mississippi, streets—even those lined with quickly constructed sandbag levees—were under several feet (meters) of water and were impassable.

Opposite:
The Mississippi River overruns its banks at Davenport, Iowa. Many towns and cities along the river were devastated by floodwaters during the summer of 1993.

It was a hot and sunny Friday in July 1993, when 12 youths from the St. Joseph's Home for Boys took a field trip to Cliff Cave County Park with 4 counselors. The park, which is located just south of St. Louis on the Mississippi River, was the perfect place for cave exploration by beginners. The waters that had flooded the Midwest were the last thing on anyone's mind.

Many areas around St. Louis—including Cliff Cave County Park—were unsafe due to the floodwaters.

CAUTION

Flood water is dangerous.
Illness and/or injury can result.

STAY BACK!

About two hours after the cave explorers had arrived at the park, the sky clouded over and there was a steady downpour that flooded the sinkholes (openings in rock formations that have been hollowed out by water) that were on top of the cave. Most of the group decided to turn back, but 5 of the youths chose to continue exploring.

Two counselors also stayed behind. The group ventured deeper inside the cave and reached a section that was only 2 feet (0.6 meters) high. To get through it, they would have to crawl on their hands and knees.

Before the 7 explorers could get through the small passageway, however, rainwater from the sinkholes above jetted into the narrow space with a sudden and powerful force that pushed them all under water.

The first victims—1 counselor and 2 boys— were found drowned in a creek just outside the cave. While rescuers feared that the rest of the group had met the same fate, some held out hope. "Well, if three are dead already, the rest are probably also dead," said Bob Cline, a cave explorer who had come out to Cliff Cave in order to help in the rescue efforts. "But, I also thought that there was a chance someone could find an air pocket and survive."

The rescue efforts continued even though the cave remained flooded. Rescuers wore diving equipment and special helmets with lanterns in order to search for the missing explorers. Another boy from St. Joseph's was found drowned 100 feet (31 meters) into the cave.

The next day, the search continued. "There's always hope. That's the only reason you go back," one grimly determined rescuer explained.

That Saturday morning, the rescuers zigzagged along the cave's waters, feeling the rocky floors in case a body had been dragged down and remained stuck under water. Nearly a half hour into the cave, some of the explorers heard a sound echoing off the walls. "I told everyone to be quiet," said Rich Schleper, a cave enthusiast who had volunteered to help with the rescue efforts. "We listened and didn't hear anything. Then we heard it again."

The sound did not seem to be coming from outside, but from somewhere in the dark depths of the underground maze. The rescuers happily cheered, "We've got a survivor!"

The survivor was 13-year-old Gary Mahr. After the flash flood had raged through the cave, Gary had managed to survive by finding air pockets that were at the cave's ceiling. He found one where he could hang on until the waters receded. "I was praying somebody would discover me. And they did," he said when he was rescued twenty hours later. When the rescuers found Gary, all his clothes—with the exception of his shorts—had been torn off by the speeding floodwaters.

Bolstered by their success, the rescuers continued their search. After a few more hours, it became apparent that Gary was the sole survivor of this tragedy. Some 150 feet (46 meters)

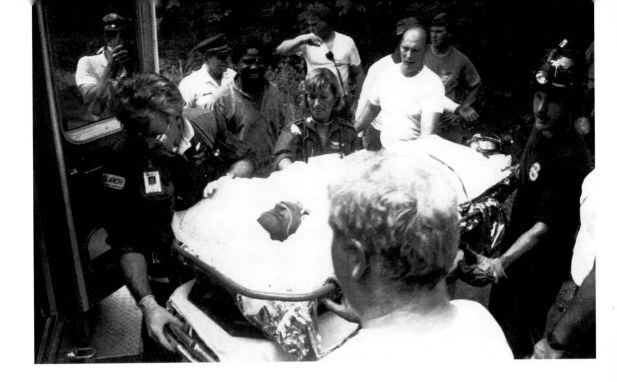

inside the cave, the last 2 victims were found. They were 21-year-old counselor Jennifer Metherd, and 12-year-old Terrill Vincent. Against all odds, Gary had survived, while 6 of his fellow explorers had perished. The toll that this flash flood took on the lives of these young people was just one small tragedy connected with the terrible floods of 1993. Other floods throughout history have also caused tragedy on a grand scale.

In the chapters that follow, we will examine the various types of floods, and their causes. We will look back at some of the worst floods in North American history and then look to the future to find out what can be done to lessen the disastrous consequences that a severe flood can bring to an area.

Thirteen-year-old Gary Mahr is placed into an ambulance by rescue workers. While exploring a cave outside St. Louis, 6 people were swept away by floodwaters, leaving only Gary alive.

What Causes Floods?

Flooding and flood damage can occur in many different ways. Sometimes floods strike without warning—and with a powerful force. At other times, they can cause damage slowly, as flood-waters may remain in certain areas for very long periods, killing crops or seeping into places that need to remain dry.

River Flooding

Unfortunately, the great Midwestern flood of 1993 was not the first time in North America's history that a swollen river overflowed its banks and caused massive destruction. In fact, river

Opposite:
Two men canoe down State Street in Montpelier, Vermont, during a 1992 flood.

flooding is the most common type of flooding in North America and has taken a tremendous toll in human life and property.

River flooding occurs when waters rise above a riverbank's level and are no longer able to be contained. In many cases, such a big rise in water levels is caused by heavy rainfall. In cold climates—mostly in the northern United States and Canada—river flooding is frequently caused by sudden thaws that melt large amounts of ice and snow within a short period of time. When a river overflows, water fills the low-lying areas that often surround its banks. These frequently flooded areas are called floodplains.

Sometimes river flooding occurs in a narrow valley. Flooding in narrow valleys is usually not prolonged, but these floodwaters can be deep and move rapidly. If flooding occurs over a flat area, a river's floodwaters may not recede for as long as several weeks. Floods over flat areas are usually shallow and the water flows slowly.

River flooding can also be caused by big ice jams. Ice floes (large pieces of ice) in a river can cause damage if and when the river begins to flood. An ice jam will cause water to rise at the point of the jam as well as upstream from it. When it breaks apart, the sudden surge of water will flood a river's banks downstream. Ice-jam floods often occur at a river's bend and

at culverts, or drainage areas, that are frozen
and do not allow the free movement of water.
Ice jams are also found near bridges or in shallow areas where a river can freeze solid.

People who live near any rivers that flood
frequently try to protect their homes by con-
structing levees—mounds of earth built along a
river's banks to control floodwaters. Levees are
the most common type of flood control in the
United States and are used mostly to protect
homes and crops. If levees are poorly designed
or maintained, flood disasters can occur, and
millions of dollars' worth of property and crops
may be damaged.

△ **13**

Flash Floods

Among the most dangerous types of floods are flash floods. During a flash flood, water levels in rivers and in streams rise rapidly. The flash flood's waters move quickly, with enough force to uproot trees and move large amounts of rock and soil. A slow-moving rainstorm can saturate an area with large quantities of precipitation in a relatively short period of time. Flash floods can be brought on by as little as a half hour's rainfall. Flash floods occur in all fifty states, but tend to happen mostly in mountainous regions. They have been known to damage populated areas where sidewalks, which cannot absorb water, speed up the flow of floodwaters.

Rescuers search for both survivors and victims after a flash flood in Shadyside, Ohio. Without warning, flash floods can sweep away people, homes, cars, animals, and trees.

Flash floods can be among the deadliest of floods because they occur rapidly. While many tragedies have been caused by sudden flash floods, some deaths might have been avoided if victims had heeded warnings (although due to the nature of this type of flooding, warnings are limited) and sought refuge on higher ground.

The National Weather Service's River and Flood Forecasting Service has a total of twelve offices throughout the country that alert people of possible flood dangers whenever possible. Their forecasts are based on meteorological data, as well as estimates of how a particular area will respond to heavy precipitation.

Dam Failures

Dam breaks are one of the most common causes of flooding. Because they hold back so much water, dams can also create potential disaster. When dams fail, they can trigger some of the largest, and most damaging floods. (In 1889, for example, a poorly maintained dam in Johnstown, Pennsylvania, was responsible for one of the most destructive floods in our nation's history.) About 20 percent of all the water that runs off the earth in North America collects in reservoirs created as a result of dam construction. For that reason, dam maintenance is important in order to avoid potential flood disasters.

Some U.S. dams—although not many—are made from concrete. Most dams in the United States are built from earth and rockfill. Maintenance crews need to be able to move the earth of a dam to create what is known as a spillway.

Spillways are built in or around a dam so that extra water can be drained. Spillways allow dam maintenance crews to control how much water is being held back in the reservoir. Since spillways are so important in preventing floods, they must always be carefully maintained.

Hurricanes and Flooding

Coastal area floods are also common. With their strong winds, hurricanes approaching coastlines will often whip up ocean tides high above normal levels. The great force of ocean waves, plus the water they carry, can cause extensive waterfront damage.

Some of the worst coastal flooding in the United States occurs during the hurricane season that lasts from June through November. The combination of strong winds and waves quickly erodes, or eats away, beaches. Beach erosion, in turn, lessens the buffer between forceful waters and coastline homes or roads. Without a buffer, water propelled by high winds can destroy homes and tear up roads and bridges. In some regions, where hurricanes are common, special hurricane barriers are often constructed for extra protection.

Just how much damage a hurricane's waves can cause often depends on the geography of the coastline. Rocky coastlines, such as those that are found in Massachusetts and Maine, often suffer less hurricane flood damage because the waves being driven onto the shore will be broken up. In parts of the northeast and northwest United States, much of the coastline is lower than the developed land around it, which also acts as a buffer. In these areas, most coastline flooding from hurricane wave action will be limited to small areas. However, in the Gulf Coast or

This house in Brooklyn, New York, suffered extensive damage during a coastal storm in 1992.

South Atlantic coastal areas—such as those in Florida—damage from hurricane waves can frequently extend 1 mile (2 kilometers) or more inland because there is no natural barrier to break their force.

Tsunamis and Tidal Waves

The seven continents sit on what are known as continental plates. Over millions of years, these continental plates have shifted. Sometimes they rub up or push against each other and cause earthquakes. Earthquakes can occur on land or under the oceans. If an earthquake is strong enough, it can even disturb ocean tides and create giant waves, called tsunamis. Coastal and undersea landslides, as well as volcanic eruptions, can also create tsunami waves.

Tsunamis are commonly called tidal waves, but they are not influenced by the gravitational pull of the moon the way tidal waves are. Tsunamis, which means "large waves in the harbor" in Japanese, are both sudden and extremely powerful. Because they cannot be predicted, they have been known to surprise coastal communities, causing great loss of life and property.

Tsunamis can travel as fast as 500 miles (805 kilometers) per hour. Shallow water causes the rapid speed of a tsunami to slow. As it slows, the tsunami wave length will shorten, while the

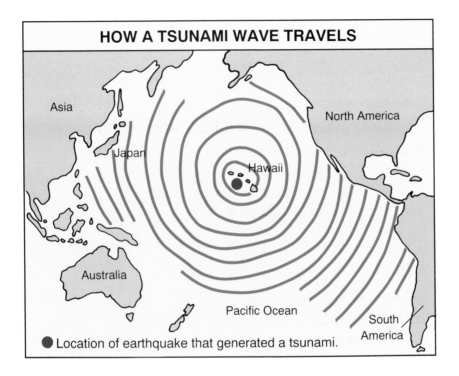

HOW A TSUNAMI WAVE TRAVELS

Asia

North America

Japan

Hawaii

Australia

Pacific Ocean

South America

● Location of earthquake that generated a tsunami.

height will increase. Some tsunamis have been nearly 100 feet (30 meters) tall. Tidal waves, which are made huge by strong winds and certain tidal conditions, can be larger but are less frequent than tsunamis.

Most tsunamis have occurred in coastal areas bordering the Pacific Ocean. The U.S. Pacific coastline, Hawaii, and Alaska have all been hit on numerous occasions by tsunami waves.

Flood-Prone Areas

Coastal storms have created both flooding and erosion problems on the Pacific Coast, where severe storms often follow one after another. Storms create similar flooding and erosion problems on the Atlantic Coast. In the northeastern coastal area of the United States, storms—which. are sometimes called Nor'easters—strike water-front communities and leave behind high tides and flooding that linger for several days.

In other regions of the United States, flood-plains surround major drainage basins (land that is drained by a river). The two most frequently flooded areas in the United States are along the Mississippi River and the central valley of California. Floodplains are also found near the Arkansas and Missouri river drainage basins. Of the 2 billion acres (1 billion hectares) of land

FLOOD CONTROL AND THE U.S. ARMY CORPS OF ENGINEERS

In the Flood Control Act of 1928, the U.S. Congress set aside $325 million for the expansion and improvement of levees along the Mississippi River. Much of the legislation was prompted by the horrific Mississippi floods that surprised the nation in 1927.

The money that was set aside in the flood control legislation was also to be used to set up a hydraulics laboratory and river gauges. The organization that was responsible for the construction of control and monitoring systems was the U.S. Army Corps of Engineers.

The control of the Mississippi River involved the construction of reservoirs and dams that could help to regulate the flow of water. The Corps is also responsible for cleaning up the Mississippi. Snags are cleared and a minimum depth of 9 feet (3 meters) is maintained with dredging equipment in order to allow for the normal passage of river traffic.

The Corps of Engineers' motto is *Essayons*—French for "let us try"—and they have been trying to control the Mississippi's waters since the Flood Control Act of 1928. The amount of money invested in the control of the Mississippi has increased since that first $325 million was set aside by Congress. Since 1928, nearly $8 billion has been spent by the Corps of Engineers in an attempt to reign in the Mississippi River with flood control devices.

that make up the United States, nearly 7 percent are subject to flooding.

While river flooding can often cause extensive damage, this type of flooding is slower than the deluge of water associated with a tsunami or a coastal storm. It may take several days of rainfall to make a river's waters jump over its banks. These extra days can mean a lot for communities that are located in a floodplain area. Damage to property and loss of life are often much less severe because people have sufficient time to prepare their homes for a flood and, if necessary, to evacuate to higher ground.

A Missouri road is impassable during a 1978 flood.

△ **21**

Great Floods in North American History

De Soto Expedition: 1539

In 1539, the first Spanish explorers, who were led by Hernando De Soto, arrived in the New World in search of gold. Their quest brought them to the Mississippi River where De Soto and his expedition decided to build boats that would carry them across the river. As they worked, they were surprised by a long and fierce spring rainfall. The heavy rains slowed the boat building efforts and the work area was quickly flooded.

Opposite:
Floodwaters in Fairbanks, Alaska, take over the downtown area in 1967. Fires ignited during flooding can cause additional damage.

As weeks went by, rain continued to soak the boatyard. Garcilaso de la Vega, one of the members of the expedition led by De Soto, remembered that the rising water "overflowed the wide level ground between the river and the cliffs that loomed some distance away; then, little by little it rose up to the top of the cliffs. Soon it began to overflow the meadows in an immense flood."

While De Soto and his expedition were not expecting them, spring floods along the Mississippi were nothing new to the Native Americans who had lived in the area for hundreds of years. Their homes were built on higher ground to avoid damage from floodwaters.

Johnstown, Pennsylvania: 1889

It is likely that no one in Conemaugh Valley, Pennsylvania, gave any thought to the first few raindrops that fell on May 30, 1889. It was Thursday, Memorial Day, and most residents had enjoyed the parades and picnics that were part of that day's celebration.

But the rain did not stop falling. By Friday morning, water from the Conemaugh River had risen several feet (meters) above the river's crest, or high point, and had begun to flood homes, stores, and factories that were downstream in the industrial town of Johnstown.

While some residents were warning people to evacuate, others were not ready to leave.

Further upstream, where the old South Fork Run dam normally held back 20 million tons (18 million metric tons) of water, the reservoir behind the dam filled up with even more water. On Friday morning, some of it began to spill over the top of the dam. By 3 P.M., the dam could not hold back the massive amounts of water. Bits and pieces of the poorly maintained dam fell away. When it broke completely, a massive wall of water rushed into the valley.

A woman stands among the debris left by the Johnstown flood of 1889. More than 2,200 people lost their lives to the raging waters.

When the dam broke, Reverend G. Brown, who was the pastor of the South Fork United Brethren Church, was there to see the water gush out. This is what he recalled:

"Having heard the rumor that the reservoir was leaking, I went up to see for myself. It was ten minutes of three. When I approached, the water was running over the breast of the dam to a depth of about a foot [0.3 meters]. The first break in the earthen surface, made a few minutes later, was large enough to admit the passage of a train of cars. When I witnessed this, I exclaimed, 'God have mercy on the people below.'"

People in Conemaugh Valley were shocked and frightened by the roaring floodwater. There was little warning as the 70-foot (21-meter) wall of water raced south on its way to Johnstown—where 30,000 people lived and worked.

As it rumbled quickly south, the floodwater destroyed everything in its path. One horrified witness described the massive wall of water as "a mist of death." Thick trees were torn from the ground and huge steam locomotives, which weighed as much as 170,625 pounds (77,385 kilograms), were hurled thousands of feet (meters) at a time. The downstream villages of South Fork and Mineral Point were completely inundated.

One farmer, who lived in the Conemaugh Valley, escaped the tide of destruction, but his wife and children were swept up by the river as it charged past their home. The water "did not come like a wave," the farmer said afterward, but "jumped on to the house and beat it to fragments" in an instant.

The wall of water hit Johnstown on Friday at 4:10 P.M. An avalanche of water and debris rushed through the streets, sweeping up people, homes, cars, and trees in its way. As the waters continued to work their way beyond Johnstown, much of the debris they had picked up was caught at a stone railroad bridge. Trees, pieces of houses, and train cars began to jam up behind the stone bridge. People swept up in

This scene depicts the situation at a stone railroad bridge where many residents of Conemaugh Valley lost their lives during the Johnstown disaster.

△ **27**

the floodwaters found themselves trapped in the wreckage. Many of them were crushed to death as additional debris continued to smash into the bridge.

More tragedy followed as the rubble at the stone bridge suddenly caught fire. Oil lamps that had been knocked over, and burning coals thrown from stoves, ignited the debris. By the time the waters had receded and the fires were put out, 2,209 people had lost their lives.

To this day, the Johnstown flood remains one of the worst disasters in North American history. The circumstances surrounding the flood remain a perfect example of the importance of proper dam maintenance. Though the rains had already caused some flooding that day, it was the failure of the dam that had unleashed the worst destruction.

Mount Landing, Arkansas: 1927

The Mississippi is the third largest river system in the world. It is fed by as many as 100,000 streams and many major tributaries, including the Missouri, the Ohio, and the Arkansas rivers. The Mississippi has always been one of the most important trade routes in America. Ever since European settlements first appeared on the Mississippi's banks, people have had to battle the river's floods with levees.

Heavy rainfall throughout the Mississippi River region began in August 1926 and did not stop until the spring of 1927. During that time, water levels in rivers that fed the Mississippi had crests of record heights. And to make matters worse, spring temperatures had begun to melt snow and ice in the north. The rivers that fed the Mississippi had channeled this additional water to the already rising river.

In April 1927, the swollen Mississippi River finally broke through a levee at Mount Landing, Arkansas. Efforts to patch up the levee with 100-pound (45-kilogram) sandbags were useless as the river's powerful water rushed through in all directions. Only moments after the river had broken through, the hole had expanded to reach almost 1 mile (2 kilometers) in width.

As the floodwaters spread, they destroyed many levees and dikes that were set up to protect communities along the Mississippi River. Within only hours of the first levee failure, homes and crops were destroyed and the Red Cross had to find temporary shelters for 325,000 people.

The floodwaters were up to 18 feet (5 meters) deep at some points. Every type of boat, from small rowboats to 700-ton (635-metric-ton) steamboats, was used by more than 33,000 rescue workers to save people—some of whom were found clinging to the remains of their homes.

When all was done, seven states were covered by floodwaters—but Louisiana, Arkansas, and Mississippi suffered the heaviest losses.

More than 300 people died in the Mount Landing flood and over half a million people lost their homes. The cost of the damage was estimated to be more than $300 million.

The Ohio and Mississippi Rivers: 1937

Heavy rains caused the Ohio River, a main tributary of the Mississippi, to rise sharply above its normal level in January 1937.

The rapidly rising river threatened the town of Cairo, Illinois, where the Ohio River and the Mississippi River meet. The Ohio's waters had risen 55 feet (17 meters) and were expected to reach 63 feet (19 meters). A levee was barely holding up against the weight of the water. The U.S. Army Corp of Engineers, working to prevent a disastrous flood, realized that they would have to divert the water to relieve some of the pressure on Cairo's levee. They successfully created a spillway by dynamiting along the river's banks.

Further south, on the Mississippi River, many engineers and volunteers worked hard to keep levees from breaking. Despite the efforts to lower the water levels upstream on the Ohio, there remained the threat of the Mississippi's

Opposite:
Months of heavy rainfall and melting snow and ice caused the Mississippi to break through levees and dikes in 1927. This photograph was taken just twenty minutes after a major break in an Arkansas levee.

△ **31**

Floodwaters wash out the approach to a bridge in 1937, and residents of Wilton, Kentucky, are transported by barge to the bridge's surface.

waters breaching, or cutting through, levees that protected New Orleans. One spillway, on the Mississippi upstream from New Orleans, was partially opened to divert more water. The water flowed into Lake Pontchartrain, outside New Orleans. The rechanneled water covered 1.25 million acres (0.5 million hectares).

While tragedy in New Orleans was successfully averted, the Ohio River flood caused 137 deaths and destroyed more than 13,000 homes.

Engineers realized that the spillways used to divert water and control the flood volume had played an important role in preventing what could have been a more widespread disaster.

The Tsunami of 1946

On April 1, 1946, an underwater earthquake shook Dutch Harbor, Alaska, which is located on a string of islands that extend from Alaska into the Pacific Ocean. Dutch Harbor suffered little damage, but huge waves caused by the quake struck hard at Hawaii and the Pacific coastline of Canada and the United States. One giant tsunami was reported by some witnesses to be as much as 100 feet (30 meters) high and to be racing at an astonishing speed of 300 miles (483 kilometers) per hour.

Gilbert Teft, a pilot for Hawaiian Airlines, had just taken off in his DC-3 airplane on a flight to Hilo, Hawaii, from Honolulu, Hawaii, when he saw the huge wave charging across the Pacific Ocean toward the Hawaiian Islands. Teft radioed what he saw to the airport and took his planeload of passengers safely to Maui, a nearby island. The first wave that crashed onto Hawaii's shores was as high as 50 feet (15 meters).

Hilo, a large waterfront city on Hawaii, was especially hard hit by the massive wave. And waterfronts on Kauai and Maui were also hit.

Small boats in the harbors were thrown onto beach homes. Large buildings were flattened by the impact of the onrushing water. In Hilo, an oil barge was thrown through a warehouse and cars, trucks, and railroad cars were tossed hundreds of feet (meters) by the raging waters. Honolulu, located on the island of Oahu, also suffered very heavy damage. In Hawaii alone, property damage was in the millions, thousands of people lost their homes, and 73 people perished when the tsunami struck.

Later, when the tsunami hit the city of San Francisco, waves reached more than 15 feet (5 meters) high. Boats were ripped from their moorings, and smaller buildings on the city's waterfront were torn from their foundations. In San Francisco, at least one person died, while in Santa Cruz, another person who was caught unaware on the beach was swept out into the ocean. All in all, the damage that the killer waves caused was totalled in hundreds of lives and millions of dollars.

Kansas-Missouri Flood of 1951

In May 1951, heavy rainfall led to a dangerous rise in the water levels of the Missouri River. By July 13, the Missouri's waters overflowed and rushed into Kansas City, an urban center with a population of 900,000. There was enough time to evacuate residents, but three of Kansas City's industrial sections were under water by the following day. An oil storage area then caught fire and firemen were called in to battle the blaze. Danger from both flooding and fire was so great that businesses were asked to close by the Kansas City mayor's office.

Kansas City, however, was not the only city caught in the flood. Nearly 20 percent of the 100,000 residents in nearby Topeka were also forced to flee their homes. And in Wichita, 337 passengers who were on a transcontinental train were stranded for nearly three days.

Seepage of muddy floodwaters into public water supplies quickly created a shortage of safe drinking water. Water had to be rationed in Kansas City.

Farmers in the region were hit exceptionally hard. Close to 850,000 acres (344,000 hectares) of wheat and corn were ruined. A good deal of livestock in Kansas City's stockyards was moved to safer grounds; however, power failures from the flood threatened the operations of many meat-packing plants that needed electrical power to run the refrigerators where they stored their products.

The floodwaters didn't stop in Kansas. Oklahoma and Missouri were also hard hit. Five days after the flood began, the U.S. government

This photograph shows a plane carrying President Harry Truman as he flew above Kansas City to survey the devastation of the 1951 Kansas-Missouri flood.

granted $25 million in federal aid to the stricken areas. The U.S. Department of Agriculture provided emergency food supplies, while special water purification systems were flown in to alleviate the shortage of fresh water. Total costs for both rescue and repair were estimated at more than $870 million.

The Tsunami of 1964

On March 27, 1964, a powerful earthquake struck Fairbanks, Alaska, killing more than 60 people, and causing tsunami warnings to be sounded all along the Pacific Coast. Because such large quantities of water are displaced during an earthquake, tsunami waves push out in all directions. Therefore, an earthquake in the northeastern part of the Pacific Ocean can create tsunamis not only in Alaska, but also in Hawaii, and along the entire west coast of the United States. In Honolulu, 300,000 residents were evacuated from their waterfront homes. On the Alaskan Gulf Coast, 6-foot (2-meter) waves tore up piers and snapped ship lines.

Two thousand miles (3,200 kilometers) away from the earthquake's epicenter (point on the surface of the land directly above the origin of an earthquake), 12-foot (4-meter) tsunami waves swamped Crescent City, California. Within minutes, downtown Crescent City was almost completely destroyed, with 12 people dead in the process. An elderly couple had drowned when they were swept out of their waterfront motel by the enormous waves. Gas tanks exploded when they were struck by the forceful waves. These explosions, in turn, caused fires to ignite and spread quickly to many near-by buildings.

Vancouver Island, off the western coast of Canada, was overrun by a 17-foot (5-meter) wave. Miraculously, no lives were lost, but the twin communities of Alberni and Point Alberni were inundated. The waves carried logs into the streets from the island's four lumber mills.

In Depoe Bay, Oregon, Mr. and Mrs. Monte G. McKenzie's children had been sleeping on a beach in a state park. As the tsunami waves rushed through, all four were swept away,

Kodiak, Alaska, was hit extremely hard by the 1964 tsunami. Boats crashed into the town, destroying several buildings.

never to be found. Their parents, sleeping in a lean-to close by, survived. "There was only a foot [0.3 meters] of air at the top of the lean-to we were in and we had to struggle to get it," Mr. McKenzie recalled. "Logs were thrown at us like matchsticks."

In Mazatlan, Mexico, located mid-coast on the Pacific side of Mexico's mainland, more than 80,000 residents and tourists fled the city with the hope of finding higher ground.

Tsunami waves created by the earthquake also struck parts of Alaska. Eleven people lost their lives after massive surges submerged Kodiak. Much of Kodiak's business district was destroyed and salmon canneries were battered beyond repair. Hundreds of fishing boats were lifted onto city streets.

Trees up to 24 inches (61 centimeters) in diameter were splintered by tsunami waves that hit Alaska in 1964.

△ 39

Nelson County, Virginia: 1969

In August 1969, storm clouds that had been part of a destructive hurricane drifted into the Blue Ridge Mountains of Virginia. Cool air from the north met the warm tropical cloud front that had been the hurricane. The result was a heavy rainfall that started to soak Virginia's Nelson County. Within six hours, about 18 inches (46 centimeters) of water fell on the area. Mountain streams and rivers overflowed. Though flash flooding was expected by local authorities, there was no time to warn the 12,000 Nelson County residents of the coming danger. They were mostly farmers scattered across the county's 471 square miles (758 square kilometers).

The flash floods hit Nelson County that night shortly after 9:30 P.M. The massive amounts of rainwater that swept through eroded the top layers of soil along the Blue Ridge Mountains. Overnight, 135 miles (217 kilometers) of roadway were quickly destroyed by flash floods and mudslides. In one area, boulders as large as 10 feet (3 meters) in diameter were thrown onto the road. In the middle of the night, one Nelson County man actually smelled the freshly torn up trees and realized that a mudslide from the flash flood might strike his home. He woke his family and they escaped to higher ground. Many people, however, were not so lucky.

All together, 250 lives were lost in the Nelson County flash flood; some of the deaths were attributed to drowning and others were due to suffocation in the mudslides. Rescue workers found one couple caught in mud up to their necks, but could not dig them out in time. And another unfortunate victim was found buried under 12 feet (4 meters) of sand.

John's Pool Room, in Scottsville, Virginia, is inundated by a flash flood in 1969.

△ **41**

1993 FLOODS IN MEXICO

Twelve days of heavy rains soaked the border town of Tijuana, Mexico, claiming 30 to 35 lives and causing $40 million in damages. The rain had Tijuana councilman Jose Cervantes Govea praying that the downpour would stop. "We wish God wouldn't send us any more rain.... We don't want any more."

There are about 30 canyons that make up the Tijuana River watershed (the total area from which water drains into a waterway) and much of the town's population lives in these canyons. Flood conditions were worsened when the houses located in the canyons blocked the natural flow of water. Hillside housing developments were subject to mudslides. Storm drainage did not work properly. The debris rushing down the canyons swept up anyone caught in its path.

The mudslides also destroyed several bridges and roads, causing transportation problems. The unpaved streets of Tijuana became rivers and were carved up by the mud flows, leaving many people stranded.

Tijuana was not alone. The mudslides brought about by rain struck all across Mexico's Baja peninsula. In Ensenada, the Mexican Army had to be called in to rescue 400 people, many of them Americans, after they had been stranded by the swollen Santo Domingo River. Flooding and mudslides had washed out the only bridge over the Santo Domingo. At Ensenada, cars and trucks mired in the mud that had overrun the roads had to be rescued by tractors. Anyone who needed to get across the Santo Domingo had to hitch their vehicle to a tractor and brave the river's rapids.

Tijuana, Mexico.

The Midwest Flood of 1993

"Help Wanted. No Experience Needed. Flexible hours. Fringe Benefits: Meals and Drink, Tetanus Shots, Band-Aids. Apply Within." This was the text of a sign that hung right outside a Ste. Genevieve, Missouri, school during the summer of 1993. Help was needed to shore up levees with sandbags in order to protect the historic town from the raging Mississippi River. The call for help was answered; 1,200 volunteers came to the 250-year-old town—some all the way from Denver, Colorado, and Memphis, Tennessee. The volunteers piled close to 40,000 sandbags onto the levee each day. By Sunday, July 18, the town's levee was reinforced by 750,000 sandbags.

Ste. Genevieve was not alone in its battle against the record 1993 floods that soaked the American Midwest. Small communities and large cities alike were battling record flooding that summer. Some researchers have said that flooding of this magnitude had not been seen in the Midwest for 1,000 years. Many people who lived along the Mississippi respected its might and were awed by the floods. Brad Bowers, a fisherman living in Iowa, noted "when you live on the river you learn to respect it and you learn that you can't predict it. The river is boss. But I've never seen it this angry."

During the Midwest floods of 1993, people worked tirelessly in an effort to control the raging rivers. In Prairie du Rocher, Illinois, residents and volunteers from around the state helped stack sandbags to reinforce a levee protecting the downtown area.

During the early summer, heavy rains bombarded much of the Midwest for five weeks straight. By July, emergency conditions existed. Satellite pictures showed that an area more than twice as large as the state of New Jersey was covered or entirely soaked by water.

The Mississippi was not the only river to jump its banks that summer. The Iowa, Minnesota, Missouri, and Des Moines rivers—all of which feed into the Mississippi—were also overflowing.

Hardest hit were farmers whose fields were located on the Mississippi's floodplain—a flat area that has excellent planting conditions due to its rich soil. Hundreds of farmers saw million-dollar crops destroyed in just a matter of days. Existing crops were swamped, while crops such as soybeans had to be planted very late in the season. Some farmers were unable to plant their soybean crops at all. Hay and alfalfa—which are used to feed livestock—were also ruined.

And some losses for farmers did not end when the floodwaters receded and the soil dried. Many farmers were not able to clean up their fields, repair farm machinery, or rebuild broken levees in time to plant crops for a 1994 harvest. Without that harvest, most farmers had little chance of thriving.

Surveying the damage and offering support to flood victims, U.S. Vice President Gore was surprised at just how much land was covered by water. "What looks like a huge river was mostly farmland. You don't realize it until you see a barn sticking up.... It's as if another Great Lake has been added to the map of the United States."

The record rainfall of summer 1993 caused other disruptions. Swollen rivers blanketed many roads with water, while some bridges

There were 13 deaths in Missouri before the Mississippi and its tributaries began to recede. Iowa, Illinois, and Minnesota each had 3 fatalities, while Wisconsin and Nebraska had only 1 death each. Crop damage was believed to be in the hundreds of millions of dollars and property damage in the billions of dollars.

FIGHTING FLOODWATERS WITH SANDBAGS

Sandbags were needed as a weapon against the record Midwest floods of 1993. The most effective sandbag for battling floods is used by the U.S. Army Corps of Engineers and is made of a type of woven plastic that holds 40 pounds (18 kilograms) of soil or sand. Plastic garbage bags and burlap sacks have also been used as sandbags.

When floods were fought with burlap bags, the bags were left to decompose. But today's plastic sandbags can't be left lying around, so heavy machinery, such as front-end loaders, is used to move the bags to a local landfill where they are broken down by road grading equipment. However, it was difficult to find enough landfill space for the massive quantities of sandbags needed to battle the 1993 floods. It remains to be seen if other ways will be developed to clean up the sandbags.

In the 1993 Midwest floods, sandbag teams had to worry not only about strong currents and raging floodwaters, there were also unseen dangers lurking in the water. Caught up in the flood was a mixture of raw sewage, industrial waste, and a variety of pesticides used by farmers. The floodwaters provided the perfect breeding ground for harmful bacteria.

For sandbaggers working in the dirty waters there was constant danger of contracting tetanus. Tetanus is a disease that can cause muscle contractions and death. It is usually contracted by drinking unclean water. While most sandbaggers were cautious and drank only bottled water, they were still in danger of contracting tetanus through cuts while working in the dirty water. To counter the threat of tetanus, sandbag teams were treated with tetanus vaccines by local health departments.

Several important issues were raised during the Midwest floods of 1993. Have too many of the Mississippi River's lands been drained for farming and development? Has the river been regulated too much by the Army Corps of Engineers? Should it be allowed to follow its normal flow patterns more often? These are just some of the questions that have been asked to date. Similar issues will surely be considered in the future when communities examine their flood preparedness, or plan to construct new riverside developments.

National Guard helicopter crewmen drop sandbags in East Carondelet, Illinois, to troops who were trying to fix a break in a levee.

△ **49**

SEMICONDUCTOR CIRCUITS, INC.
HAVERHILL, MASS.
POWER SOURCE
SW12-5S1000

Forecasting and Facing Floods

Floods are one of the many natural occurrences over which we have little control. They play an important part in the natural cycle of life. While a flood can cause a lot of damage to a farmer's field, a flood can also carry important minerals and nutrients from mountain slopes to valleys and enrich the soil.

The Native Americans whom the Spanish explorers encountered along the Mississippi were familiar with the river's behavior. If the Mississippi began to threaten homes on higher

Opposite:
A meteorologist checks a flood prevention monitor that has been placed along the Arkansas River.

These effigy mounds, called Marching Bears, are located at Effigy Mounds National Monument in Iowa, and were built by Native Americans to escape rising floodwaters.

ground, the Native Americans would construct huge mounds of dirt where they could seek refuge. Some of these mounds were still in existence when the Mississippi overflowed in 1926-1927. Cattle caught in the river's flood found safety on top of these mounds.

The Study of Water

The study of water is known as hydrology, and scientists who study water are called hydrologists. Hydrologists work closely with engineers in order to develop effective flood control systems. Some hydrologists construct models of streams or rivers and flood them to see where and how the greatest flood damage occurs. Spillway and levee systems are also tested this way. Even rainstorms are created in special laboratories to determine how absorbent different types of soil are, and how quickly a flood can develop under certain rainfall conditions.

The first person to keep an official record of a river's water levels was William Kelker. He lived in Pennsylvania and kept records of this kind on the Susquehanna River. Kelker used an old bridge pier near the city of Harrisburg, on which he painted height measurements. He used

AVERTING A TRAGEDY

It was a fast-thinking hydrologist in Bloomfield, Connecticut, who first noticed just how drenching the rainfall was on April 9, 1980. He was a specialist in flash floods, and the large amounts of rain signaled to him that there was a strong possibility of flash flooding in the low-lying areas of Connecticut near the Housatonic River.

The hydrologist checked rain gauges throughout the area and saw that the rainfall was indeed heavy. In Hartford, the capital of Connecticut, some streams were already overflowing and rain gauge warning systems were sounding off. After studying the overflow patterns, he called the Bridgeport office of the National Weather Service to warn them.

But forecasters did not think that the weather was dangerous enough to sound an alarm to communities that were in low-lying areas, which included Bridgeport.

The hydrologist saw that streams feeding the Housatonic River continued to overflow and a few hours later he called the National Weather Service again. This time they agreed that there was the danger of flash flooding. A warning was given to residents that very evening at 11:45 P.M., and some communities were evacuated.

The determined hydrologist used his knowledge to save many lives. Although property damage was in the millions of dollars, only one life was lost. If special action had not been taken, loss of life could have been much greater.

this gauge to record the levels of the Susquehanna River from 1874 to 1893.

Today, a river's water levels are monitored with sophisticated equipment. Mr. Kelker's primitive instrument for the Susquehanna has been replaced by a gauge that is operated by the U.S. Geological Survey, in cooperation with both the National Weather Service and the Philadelphia Electric Company. This new measuring device transmits a report of the river's water levels every three hours to a satellite that is orbiting the Earth.

Official weather forecasts are gathered from many weather stations throughout the world that work together in tracking weather formations. The National Weather Service, which is based in Washington, D.C., is just one of many organizations that follow up on any new developments in the weather. The National Weather Service watches the Northern Hemisphere very closely with high speed computers that are able to assess changes in weather on an hourly basis. The National Weather Service can also give meteorologists an idea of the weather conditions for as many as ten days in advance. However, even the short-term forecasts can be tricky, as tiny changes in weather patterns or local influences in a given geographical location can throw off predictions.

After the river level data is transmitted to the satellite, it is then re-transmitted to the U.S. Geological Survey, the National Weather Service Forecast Center, and the U.S. Army Corps of Engineers.

Meteorologists (scientists who specialize in analyzing weather data) and hydrologists use many different types of devices to measure rainfall. The simplest way to do this is with a pan-funnel-cylinder gauge that uses a dipstick. The pan-funnel-cylinder device is accurate, but it does not allow meteorologists to study widespread rainfall levels.

To measure rainfall over a broad area, some meteorologists and hydrologists use automated weighing or tipping-bucket types of gauges. Both of these instruments are connected to

A meteorologist loads weather data into a computer that is part of an automatic weather monitoring station.

△ 55

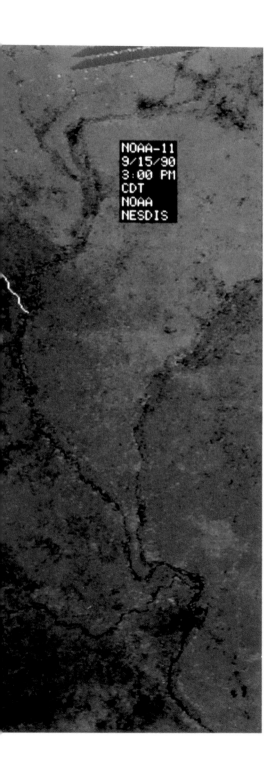

NOAA-11
9/15/90
3:00 PM
CDT
NOAA
NESDIS

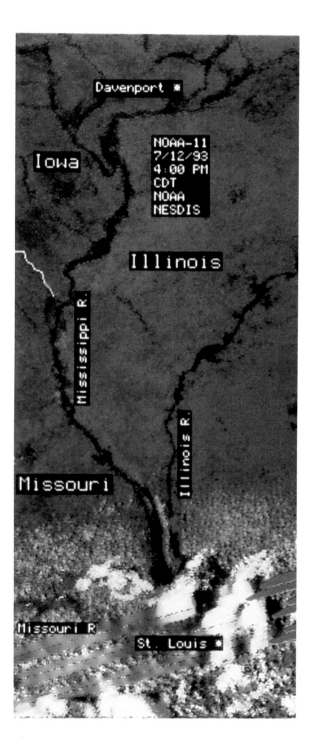

Davenport ✶

Iowa

NOAA-11
7/12/93
4:00 PM
CDT
NOAA
NESDIS

Illinois

Mississippi R.

Illinois R.

Missouri

Missouri R

St. Louis ✶

telephone lines that run to a weather service's office. In the office, the meteorologist can dial a special number assigned to each gauge and obtain a reading of rainfall levels. These automated gauges have also been linked to satellites in order to be able to monitor rainfall levels more quickly and efficiently.

Being Prepared for a Flood

As we have seen, floods can occur in a large variety of ways. Some of our nation's worst flooding incidents could have been prevented, but many other types of flood disasters—such as those that resulted from the heavy Midwest rainfall of 1993—simply could not have been avoided. The best way to meet the challenges of natural floods is to learn more about them, learn how to adapt to them, and study various ways to be prepared in case a flood does occur. The following basic guidelines for responding to a flood disaster have been established by the American Red Cross:

"Your home has been flooded. Although floodwaters may be down in some areas, many dangers still exist. Here are things to remember in the days ahead:
- Roads may be closed because they have been damaged, or are covered by water. Barricades may have been placed for your

△ **57**

This flood gauge near Big Bend National Park in Texas is used to show the depth water can reach during flash floods in otherwise dry areas.

protection. If you come upon a barricade or a flooded road, go another way.

- Keep listening to the radio for news about what to do, where to go, or places to avoid.

- Emergency workers will be assisting people. You can help them by staying off roads and out of the way.

- If you must walk or drive in areas that have been flooded, stay on firm ground. Moving water only 6 inches (15 centimeters) deep can sweep you off your feet. Standing water may be electrically charged from underground or downed power lines.

- Flooding may have caused familiar places to change. Floodwaters often erode roads and walkways. Flood debris may cover animals and broken glass, and it's also very slippery. Avoid walking through it.
- Play it safe. Additional flooding or flash floods can occur. Listen for local warnings and information. If your car stalls in rapidly rising waters, get out immediately and climb to higher ground.
- Be prepared. If you are asked to evacuate you should have the following supplies ready:
  - a battery operated radio and extra batteries
  - a flashlight
  - a first aid kit and any necessary medications
  - one gallon of water, and a three-day supply of nonperishable food per person."

We have learned that floods can occur anywhere, at almost any time. They can happen surprisingly fast, or gradually, over a period of time. In either case, the potential for destruction is great. Only through increased awareness of flood dangers and careful preparation can citizens and communities hope to lessen the disastrous effects floods may bring.

Glossary

breach A hole made by water that cuts through a levee or dam.

chasm A deep crack in the earth's surface.

crest The high point of a river.

culvert A pipelike drainage area underneath a roadway.

dipstick A graduated rod for measuring quantity or depth.

effigy mounds Huge mounds of dirt built by Native Americans to escape high floodwaters.

epicenter The area of the earth's surface directly above the place of origin of an earthquake.

erosion A washing away of the soil and rock of the earth's surface.

flash flood A sudden, violent flood.

floodplain The low-lying area that often surrounds a river bank and is frequently flooded.

hydrologist A scientist who studies water.

levee An embankment built alongside a river to prevent flooding.

lock An enclosure in a waterway that allows the water level to be changed in order to let ships pass through.

meteorologist A scientist who specializes in analyzing weather data.

sinkhole An opening in a rock formation that has been hollowed out by water.

spillway A channel made for draining excess water.

tributary A river or stream that flows into a larger body of water.

tsunami A giant wave that is caused by an earthquake or shifting of the earth.

watershed The total area from which water drains into a waterway.

Further Reading

Ayer, Eleanor. *Our Great Rivers and Waterways.* Brookfield, CT: Millbrook Press, 1994.

Cooper, J. *Dams.* Vero Beach, FL: Rourke, 1991.

Fradin, Dennis. *Floods.* Chicago, IL: Childrens Press, 1982.

Hester, Nigel. *The Living River.* New York: Franklin Watts, 1991.

Knapp, Brian. *Flood.* Austin, TX: Raintree Steck-Vaughn, 1990.

Lampton, Christopher. *Tidal Wave.* Brookfield, CT: Millbrook Press, 1992.

HAVE YOU EVER FACED A DISASTER?

If you have ever had to be brave enough to face a flood, you probably have a few exciting stories to tell! Twenty-First Century Books invites you to write us a letter and share your experiences. The letter can describe any aspect of your true story—how you felt during the disaster; what happened to you, your family, or other people in your area; or how the disaster changed your life. Please send your letter to Disaster Editor, TFCB, 115 West 18th Street, New York, NY 10011. We look forward to hearing from you!

Source Notes

Adler, Jerry. "Troubled Waters," *Newsweek*, July 26, 1993.

"Alaska Is Struck By Severe Quake; 60 Feared Dead," *The New York Times*, March 28, 1964.

Blair, William. "West Coast Hit By Tidal Waves," *The New York Times*, March 29, 1964.

Booth, Cathy. "Catastrophe 101," *Time*, September 14, 1992.

Casteneda, Carol. "Disease Concerns Rise Along With the Water," *USA Today*, July 8, 1993.

_____. "Disease Months in Making," *USA Today*, July 8, 1993.

Church, George J. "Flood, Sweat and Tears," *Time*, July 26, 1993.

Clark, Champ, and the Editors of Time Life Books. *Planet Earth: Flood.* Alexandria, VA: Time Life Books, 1982.

Dvorchak, Robert J., and the Associated Press. *The Flood of '93.* New York: St. Martin's Press, 1993.

Fedarko, Kevin. "After the Deluge: Health Hazards," *Time*, July 26, 1993.

Federal Interagency Floodplain Management Task Force. *Floodplain Management in the United States: An Assessment Report.* Washington, D.C.: 1992.

Golden, Tim. "After the Deluge, Tijuana's Future is Dimmer," *The New York Times*, February 1, 1993.

Goldberg, Laura. "Damage, Deaths Climb; More Rain Expected," *USA Today*, July 13, 1993.

_____. "What Else Could Possibly Go Wrong," *USA Today*, July 13, 1993.

Goldberg, Laura, and Robert Davis. "Punishing Rain, Heat Continue," *USA Today*, July 8, 1993.

MacMillan, Richard. "79 Dead in Hawaii," *The New York Times*, April 2, 1964.

Mathews, Tom. "What Went Wrong," *Newsweek*, September 7, 1992.

Morganthau, Tom. "Storm Warnings," *Newsweek*, September 14, 1992.

Turner, Wallace. "Guard Patrolling Anchorage; City Lacks Water and Power," *The New York Times*, March 28, 1964.

Index

△ **63**

Acknowledgements and Photo Credits

Cover: Gillette/Liaison USA; p. 4: ©Larry Mayer/Gamma Liaison Network; pp. 6, 44, 47, 49: Reuters/Bettmann; pp. 9, 22: AP/Wide World Photos; p. 10: ©Sandy Macys/ Gamma Liaison Network; p. 13: ©Don Jones/Liaison USA; p. 14: ©Mark Burnett/ Photo Researchers, Inc.; p. 17: ©Rafael Macia/Photo Researchers, Inc.; p. 21: L & D Klein/Photo Researchers, Inc.; pp. 25, 32: UPI/Bettmann Newsphotos; p. 27: Bettmann; p. 30: The Bettmann Archive; pp. 36, 41: UPI/Bettmann; p. 38: Kodiak Historical Society; p. 39: United States Geological Survey; p. 42: ©Robert Walchli/ Gamma Liaison Network; p. 50: ©Lowell Georgia/Photo Researchers, Inc.; p. 52: Effigy Mounds National Monument/National Park Service; p. 55: ©David Parker/ Science Photo Library/Photo Researchers, Inc.; p. 56: NOAA/Science Source/Photo Researchers, Inc.; p. 58: ©Björn Bölstad/Photo Researchers, Inc.
Art by Blackbirch Graphics, Inc.